Jefferson County Library
620 Cedar Avenue
Port Hadlock, WA 98339
(360) 385-6544 www.jclibrary.info

Daisy and the Egg

by Jane Simmons

 Little, Brown and Company
Boston   New York   London

To my dad

First published in Great Britain in 1998 by Orchard Books

First U.S. Paperback Edition

Library of Congress Cataloging-in-Publication Data
Simmons, Jane.
    Daisy and the Egg / Jane Simmons. — 1st U.S. ed.
        p.   cm.
    Summary: Daisy the duckling eagerly awaits the arrival of a
new brother or sister, even helping Mama Duck sit on the egg while
they wait for it to hatch.
    ISBN 0-316-79747-2 (hc) / ISBN 0-316-73872-7 (pb)
    [1. Ducks — Infancy — Fiction. 2. Animals — Infancy —
Fiction. 3. Eggs — Fiction. 4. Brothers and Sisters — Fiction.]
I. Title.
PZ7.S59182Dai   1998
[E] — dc21   98-35949

HC: 10 9 8 7 6 5 4 3
PB: 10 9 8 7 6 5 4 3 2 1

SC

Printed in Singapore

"How many eggs now?" asked Daisy.
"Four," Aunt Buttercup said proudly. "My
three and Mama's green one."
"Your aunt's sitting on an egg for me,"
explained Mama Duck.
"Can I sit on one, too?" asked Daisy excitedly.

It wasn't easy.

Every day, Mama Duck
sent Daisy over with
food for Aunt Buttercup.

Daisy listened as the chicks
tapped softly inside their shells.
"You'll have a brother or sister
soon," said Aunt Buttercup.
Daisy was so excited.

When Daisy and Mama Duck went to visit Aunt Buttercup the next day, she was flapping her wings.

"They're hatching! They're hatching!" she called.

One of Aunt Buttercup's ducklings had cracked its shell. Daisy watched her first cousin struggle out.

"Yuck! He's all wet!" said Daisy.
"Shhh!" scolded Mama Duck.
Then Aunt Buttercup's other two
ducklings hatched.

While Mama Duck and Aunt Buttercup talked about names, Daisy waited for Mama's egg. She thought she heard something . . . but nothing happened.

They all listened . . . but still
there was no sound from the egg.

That night, Mama Duck sat on her egg, but the next day, it still hadn't hatched.

"Some eggs just don't hatch," said Mama Duck. "Come and play with your cousins, Daisy."

But Daisy wanted to stay with Mama's egg.

Daisy made a hole in the feathers, rolled the egg in, and sat on top. "Come along, Daisy!" called Mama Duck. But Daisy wouldn't move.

It was getting dark, and
Daisy was cold and tired.

Mama Duck came back.
"We'll sit together until
morning," she said kindly.
"Yes," said Daisy.

Pip! Pip! Pip! Daisy
woke up. It was the egg!

Her new brother struggled out
of his shell and said, "Pip! Pip!"
"Quack!" said Daisy.
"Pip!" he said again.
"Pip!" said Daisy.
"Hello, Pip," said Mama Duck.

And together they
watched the sun rise on
Little Pip's hatching day.